Buzzby Bee

Rich Riffle

NEWMAN SPRINGS PUBLISHING
320 Broad Street
Red Bank, NJ 07701

First originally published by Newman Springs Publishing 2020

ISBN 978-1-64531-029-7 (Paperback)
ISBN 978-1-64531-030-3 (Digital)

Printed in the United States of America

To my lovely wife Diane and my cherished friend Dixee.

HIVE ELEMENTARY

1

Our tale begins in a large cherry orchard, not unlike many such well-tended and thriving orchards found across the land. In this one, however, lives a small brave young bee destined to unite with mankind in a way never seen before or since.

It was a cool spring morning at Buzzby's hive, which was shaped like a huge football wrapped in thin brown–gray paper. His hive was one of many in the orchard and was located not far from the outer edge of the plantation. Though somewhat isolated from the other hives, members of Buzzby's colony often had contact with the other colonies to coordinate pollen gathering activites and participate in social events.

Buzzby and his friends: Leezl, Stinger, and Zeebert were playing around their cherry tree before school. They were outside the home of retired colonel William Beesly, an old Dive Stinger Bee who had met a terrible fate in his younger days. The members of the colony called him One-Wing Willie, a nickname he accepts with pride and honor.

"Hey! One-Wing," Zeebert shouted teasingly. "Come on out and fly with us!" Zeebert was stalky in stature with a strong desire to someday join the ranks of the soldier bees. He was the troublemaker of the group; his antics were at times questioned by the elders.

"Come on, Zzeebert. Quit picking on Miszzter Willie," Buzzby said with his changing, high-pitched adolescent voice. His lisping speech showed his youth which was evident in all immature young bees. "It'zz time to go to szzchool." Buzzby was a chubby cherub-faced bee whose wings had not grown at the same rate as the rest of his body. His antennae were still developing. "Let'zz go or we'll be late. You know how Mizz Honey getzz."

"Yes, let us go," said Princess Leezl in a soft persuasive tone. Leezl, the queen's daughter, was tall and fair with beautiful black-and-gold spots on her wings and more black stripes on her body than most other bees. All in the orchard's colonies considered her to be quite lovely. She was a voice of reason and considered quite proper for her age.

Stinger flew just ahead of the four friends; he was thin with long antennae and round black-rimmed glasses. He always considered the consequences of his actions and many thought he would grow up to be an attorney bee or the head of a pollen trading company.

Miss Honey, a pleasant long, slender teacher bee—the favorite of all the students—was at the door of the school as she greeted the four friends. "Zeebert, I watched as you annoyed Mr. Willie," she said in a soft tone. "He's been through a great deal in his life. You could learn a lot from such a great bee. Show respect for your elders." Zeebert bowed his head, faking shame, as he went to his seat. Miss Honey shook her head in discontent.

The day went by much as any other school day for the children. Lessons in reading, writing, math, as well as pollen gathering and flight control were normal for the youth of the colony. After school, the sun was high in the sky. The air was warm with a slight breeze. Buzzby asked Leezl if he could fly her home which she gladly accepted. Leezl liked Buzzby, though he was not a popular sports bee nor did he particularly aspire to be a soldier bee. He was kind, gentle, and polite—qualities Leezl

admired. As the two of them flew through the cherry orchard they could smell the sweet blossoms and enjoyed the warm afternoon breeze. They would fly up, down, and all around the blossom-covered branches of the cherry trees. At times they would fly near the ground to feel the coolness of the grass and moist soil, occasionally landing on a dandelion to rest.

They stopped along the way and admired the concentration and precision of the worker bees gathering pollen. The worker bees were professional gatherers. As they crawl around on a bloom, pollen sticks to the hairs on their bodies which is then brushed by their middle legs down to their pollen baskets on their hind legs. The pollen is used to feed the colony which helps the hive grow strong. Buzzby and Leezl liked to fly from blossom to blossom. Occasionally, they would jokingly dive bomb their favorite officer soldier bee, Captain

Comb, who was going to marry Miss Honey. He held the position of captain of the Royal Guard, a prestigious position for a soldier bee. He was a handsome slender officer, fierce when needed but generally kind and thoughtful. For a Soldier Bee, he was always quick with a joke or two of his own and did not seem to mind these meddlesome youngsters.

When Buzzby and Leezl arrived home they agreed to call on their friends Zeebert and Stinger after dinner. The four met just outside the hive. "I can't be gone long," Stinger said with a smile. "I have homework to do."

"Me too," Zeebert said with a scowl. "Miss Honey gave me extra homework for being rude to One-Wing. I have to write a paper on hovering and practice my flight patterns." Even with his extra homework, Zeebert suggested they had enough time to fly to the edge of the orchard to Pollen

Plaza, a place he would occasionally sneak off to while his friends did their homework or chores.

Pollen Plaza was the name of the largest and oldest tree in the orchard. It was located at the edge of the orchard, the last tree before the barren fields beyond. It's moss covered, twisted, and crooked branches made it look haunted. The great tree was neglected though it was not dead. Hanging from many of its branches were remnants of a number of old hives long since abandoned and broken, many nearly rotted completely, black and moldy and no longer able to support life. Most now merely served as a sad reminder of days long since gone. In its prime Pollen Plaza was the main tree for orchard wide activities such as commerce and entertainment for all of the colonies. It also served as a meeting place for bees of the orchard and visitors from other lands. At its peak, Pollen Plaza was the center of the pollen trade industry with vibrant stores, the popular Beezjou theater, the celebrated nightclub Combacabana, and business centers where the pollen trade was active.

Leezl, however, reminded Zeebert of the Royal Rule about not going to the Edge or the Plaza. The Royal Rule was issued by the Council of Queens, which Leezl's mother leads, after the War of the Fog when she decreed the edge of the orchard, often referred to simply as the Edge, as dangerous to all bees and banned all from the area. Suddenly, a voice boomed from above giving the young bees a start. "Don't go there you tiny fliers," warned the scratchy voice of One-Wing Willie. "The Edge is very dangerous. Those who go there never come back," he said slowly with a slightly sinister voice.

Stinger, startled and trembling, said, "Oh! Mr. Willie, you scared us!" After catching his breath he asked, "Mr. Willie, would you please tell us what really happened during the War of the Fog?"

Colonel "One-Wing" Beesly grunted and moved slowly to settle down on a cherry blossom. The youngsters gathered at his feet and listened excitedly to the decorated veteran Dive Stinger Bee. He began his story by telling them of the good ole days when beautiful, sweet, colorful wildflowers surrounded the orchard. Worker bee leaders from colonies all over the orchard would assemble at Pollen Plaza to plan their pollen gathering day, making sure that all the hives shared equally in the abundant treasure. With a slight whisper and wide open eyes, he said, "Then one summer, a strange fog appeared from far across the fields. Worker bees were gathering pollen from the fields of flowers when the fog floated overhead and settled down around them. Many bees fell to the ground sick, unable to fly and died in that terrible fog. Luckily, some were able to return and warn the hives of the orchard of the mysterious fog." With their eyes wide open and their jaws dropping the youngsters listened intently to his every word as he told them how the queens from all over the orchard convened a Council of Queens and declared war on the fog. The generals from all the hives gathered to plan a counterattack. They assembled their soldier bees and dive stingers. "Thousands of soldier bees and dive stingers from all over the orchard formed squadrons to go beyond the Edge to battle the fog, few returned," he said in a slow, deep tone.

He went on to tell them that he led one of the Dive Stinger squadrons. His was assigned to swarm high over the fields to get to the far side of the fog and attack from the rear. Other squadrons were assigned to swarm and attack the flanks. Reliving the experience, One-Wing said, "Then we saw it! The strange, hideous giant creature, called human." His emotions could be heard in his voice.

"Humans have no wings, they only have four legs but only use two to walk. The other legs waved in the air which had somehow made the dangerous and deadly fog."

His squadron swarmed in and attacked the human, stinging it several times. "Just then," said One-Wing, "the human swung at me striking a mighty blow. I crashed to the ground where it stepped on me; many bees of the orchard were badly injured or died in the attack. I was a lucky one, severely injured with crushed wings. All the squadrons suffered heavy casualties."

With a softened voice, he explained how he could hardly move but somehow managed to take cover under a nearby leaf. After a while, he saw that the fog had lifted, and the human was gone. He knew he had to get back to warn the colony and be with his family. He gathered the strength to begin his dangerous long journey across the field. As he crawled over rocks, under twigs, and around weeds, he came across other soldier bees and dive stingers who lay injured. Unable to help them return home, he made as many as possible comfortable knowing that help would soon arrive. One-Wing told the youngsters that many of those who returned were able to continue as soldier bees and dive stingers, while others moved on to work, live, and contribute to their respective colonies, just like he had. Colonel Beesly continued his story. He managed to crawl his way back to the edge of the orchard where he joined others who had been rescued. The rescue bees were busily finding and returning many war bees to home. While in the hospital, his left wing was removed because it was crushed; but his right wing, though useless for flight, was saved. "Now you know where I got the name," Willie said.

The youngsters learned that the loses during the War of the Fog were so great that several of the orchards' colonies had to join together to survive. "Thankfully," One-Wing said. "Pollen Plaza had been evacuated so no civilian bees were harmed. However, the fog stuck to the structures making them unusable," he said solemnly. "The Council of Queens had no choice but to declare Pollen Plaza a hazardous area, and everything was condemned. With no one able to go there, the plaza fell to ruin, shriveled, wilted, and rotted. The Queen then issued the Royal Rule, no one was to fly to the Edge or go near Pollen Plaza." With a tear in his eye, he continued, "Ever since that battle with the fog, the luscious smelling roses, crocus, snapdragons, and other colorful flowers that once fed the hives in and around the orchard have died off. The fields of sunflowers also died off leaving only the weed-filled, dry, barren land beyond the orchard."

Buzzby inquisitively asked, "Why don't they teach uszz about thizz in szzchool, Mr. Willie?"

One-Wing replied, "Because of the Royal Rule. As bees were forbidden to go to the Edge or beyond, the Council of Queens and the school elders decided it was more important to focus on the future and the teachings on bee life. Due to the devastation from the War of the Fog, they also decided to remove all references to humans in your books and libraries. They believed this would protect the youth of the colonies."

Buzzby wisely said, "I'm not szzo szzure that wazz a good idea."

Col. William Beesly reflectively said, "It was at the time, my young flyer. It was at the time."

Zeebert smirked. "Yeah, yeah, yeah. But that war was a long time ago. I think it's about time we go to the Edge and see for ourselves. I mean, what's the big deal now?"

Leezl cautiously reasoned, "I do not think we should disobey my mother's rule. We could get into deep trouble. Besides, we have plenty of things to do right around here, like play-acting as soldier bees or learning from the pollen gatherers."

"Yeah! Zzeebert," said Buzzby. "It'zz time to go now. I have chorezz to do and you, Zzeebert, have plenty of eggzztra homework to do." Thinking only of the trouble they may get into, Buzzby flew away as quickly as he could.

"Wait for us, Buzzby," Stinger shouted. "Leezl and I are right behind you. You comin' Zeebert?" Zeebert begrudgingly followed as they flew home for the night.

The next day was an unusually warm day for spring. The worker and soldier bees were moving slower than usual because of the heat. The children were sent home early from school as the heat made concentrating on their lessons more difficult. This gave Miss Honey some extra time to prepare for her marriage to the dashing Captain Comb. The wedding was to be quite the event since Captain Comb was the leader of the Royal Guard and thus deserving of the queen's presence.

"Hey, gang! Follow me! I got a surprise for ya," Zeebert said excitedly as he gingerly flew out the schoolroom door. His friends could tell he was up to one of his capers. Buzzby and Leezl hesitated while Stinger cautiously thought about the idea, but they slowly followed their friend with childlike curiosity.

"Where we going, Zzeebert?" asked Buzzby. "Szzlow down, you know I can't fly that fazzst."

"Oh, come on. This'll do ya good," said Zeebert tauntingly. "Heck, it might even help you shed off some of that beebee fat."

Leezl kindly said, "Please do not tease Buzzby, Zeebert. He's doing the best he can." She turned and gave Buzzby a smile.

They were so distracted by Zeebert's enthusiasm and teasing of Buzzby they had not noticed the direction they were going. Suddenly, Stinger screamed, "WAIT! We're at the EDGE! We're at POLLEN PLAZA! Let's get outta here!"

They swerved and landed on a brittle branch deep within the forbidden, scary old cherry tree. Buzzby, Leezl, and Stinger had never been this far from their hive before. Leezl tried to reason with Zeebert. "Zeebert, this was a bad idea and is in direct violation of my mother's rule."

Angrily, Stinger said, "We could get in big trouble, Zeebert. We should not be here." Zeebert seemed to be uncaring about the rule or what trouble they could get into. He was not going to leave without first looking around.

Trembling with fear trying to catch his breath Buzzby said, "Thizz izz not good. I'm szzcared. Let'szz go."

As they argued, a strange, hypnotic, warm, gentle breeze arose quieting their voices. They looked in awe at the vast wasteland beyond the orchard. It was just as One-Wing Willie had described. Beyond the orchard, they saw no flowers, no blooms, no color, only dusty dirt and wind-tossed weeds. Zeebert was finally speechless.

Far off in the distance, they saw a strange-looking thing. It was huge! It was nothing like they had ever seen before. It was not round like their hive but square. It was brightly colored with square openings on its sides. As their courage returned, they all cautiously flew to the top of Pollen Plaza for a better look. Stinger, always a cautious but curious thinker thought out loud, "Is that a hive of some sort? What kind of hive could it be? Could it be the hive of the human One-Wing Willie talked about? It seems to be familiar to me." Recalling with an odd sense of glee, "I think it's called a house. I read an old book my grandfather had. It talked about human hives, I mean, houses." He continued to recall his reading as his friends looked at him, puzzled. "Yeah, it's a house, I'm sure of it. That must be where the human lives that started the War of the Fog. The one One-Wing Willie told us about."

Just then the giant creature came out of the large oddly shaped hive. Just as characterized by Colonel Beesly, it had four legs but walked on only two and had no wings. Human. "Let us go home," Leezl whispered as if at this distance the human could hear her. "Buzzby, please fly me home, I do not wish to stay here any longer. If Mother finds out we were here we shall be in big trouble." Buzzby and Leezl flew away together. Stinger and Zeebert left a short time later racing each other home.

Buzzby and Leezl, feeling safe on their flight home, stayed above the trees of the orchard to enjoy the view. They could see their hive in the distance and knew they would be home soon. They stopped for a moment to allow Buzzby to rest; his wings were still too small for such long flights. They talked about One-Wing Willie's story and what they had seen in the distance from Pollen Plaza. Although Leezl was saddened by Colonel Beesly's story, she could not help but wonder about the fields of flowers. "Would it not be beautiful, Buzzby? Think of all those flowers! The bright colors, the sweet smells, and the pollen. Oh, how I wish it could be that way again." Rested, they continued on home slowly while they talked. Ever mindful of her dear friend Buzzby, she said, "The wind seems to be picking up. Let us go down below the treetops where we will be protected. It should be easier for you to fly." Leezl cared for Buzzby greatly; they had known each other since they first came out of the combs as infant drones. Buzzby was not used to flying this much especially in the wind. He still found it difficult to maintain flight control. Leezl dove under a branch and giggled. She called out playfully, "Come on, Buzzby. Down here."

"Okay, here I come! Look, I'm a Dive Szztinger comin' in for the attack!" Buzzby flew higher and higher then turned as if to come straight down at Leezl just like a Dive Stinger might do when attacking a mortal enemy. A sudden gust of wind caught Buzzby and blew him off course. "HEY!" he shouted as he struggled to stabilize his flight and regain his direction. "I'm out of control!" The wind was too strong for him; he was carried farther and farther away from the safety of the trees and his friend Leezl. He was carried back to the edge of the orchard. Buzzby yelled out "Leezl, HELP! I can't szzlow down! I'm out of control!" Sadly, she could not hear him as he tumbled out of her sight toward the wasteland beyond the orchard.

"Buzzby! Where are you?" Leezl cried out in vain as she struggled to the top of a tall branch. Fighting against the strong wind, she frantically looked and looked for her friend, Buzzby. "HELP! HELP!" She called to anyone that might hear. Scared and crying, she flew as fast as she could under the cover and protection of the trees to her home hive to get help.

Zeebert and Stinger were waiting near the hive, not knowing what had happened. "Leezl, what's wrong?" asked Stinger.

Leezl was out of breath and could barely speak. "It is Buzzby. He was playing dive stinger when the wind carried him away toward the edge of the orchard. Please, we need to get help," she pleaded. They raced to see the queen.

The three stood before the queen, humbled, knowing they had violated the Royal Rule. Leezl was apprehensive as she knew her mother would be disappointed in her actions. Still, she explained Buzzby's out of control flight that took him in the direction of the forbidden wastelands. The queen was indeed disappointed, but respected Leezl's courage to come forward. She immediately summoned her generals. Two search and rescue squadrons were immediately deployed to look for Buzzby.

Meanwhile, Buzzby saw that he was over the barren wasteland. He regained enough flight control to stop tumbling but was still carried by the wind. His path was toward the strange huge hive of the giant creature, the human. For a moment, his thoughts were of One-Wing Willie and what a terrible ordeal his battle with the human must have been. The wind had carried Buzzby to the human's hive where he was able to land gasping for breath. As he rested, he cautiously looked inside the hive through one of the square openings recalling what his friend Stinger had said. This strange hive was called a house. Inside he saw brightly colored flowers. The urge to go inside the house of the human to see the flowers, smell their fragrance, and taste their pollen was overwhelming. So he cautiously slipped in through an opening.

Szztrange, he thought when he tried to land on one of the flowers. *Thizz flower is not like otherzz I have zzeen. The petalzz are flat. The flowerzz are flat. The stemzz and leavezz are flat. It'zz not fragrant, and I can't szzeem to gather itzz pollen.* As he looked around the house, he saw hundreds of flowers on the walls lining the house. Buzzby had never seen the inside of a human house; he knew nothing of wallpaper or photographs. It was only today that he learned from his friend, Stinger, that a human hive is called a house. He was amazed at the bright, beautiful colors. There was a strange aroma of something sweet in the air. It was not pollen; it was something else, something he had never experienced nor could describe. He could not understand why the inside of this human's house was so wonderful and fragrant while the outside was dreary and drab.

Without warning, a thunderous clap and a gust of wind startled Buzzby. Something had slapped the wall next to him. Frightened, he flew as fast as his little wings could carry him, looking for a safe place to land. The frightful large human was in the room yelling, "Get out, you crazy bee, GET OUT!" The human chased Buzzby around the room.

Buzzby found a safe place to land and gather his wits and courage. He said his thoughts out loud, "Why is thizz human trying to hurt me? What have I done to deszzerve thizz?" The human suddenly stopped and gazed at Buzzby with cautious curiosity and puzzlement.

The human was stunned to hear Buzzby talking to himself. The human asked, "What was that you said, little bee?"

Buzzby, surprised he could understand the human, tentatively flew closer ever mindful that the human was dangerous. Buzzby said timidly,

"Why, human? Why? Why do you want to hurt me?" In an instant, Buzzby thought of the many hive families throughout the orchard that lost loved ones during the War of the Fog. He remembered One-Wing's story that the human caused the fog. "Why did you create the fog that hurt so many bees?"

The human, still puzzled, replied, "You bees are nothing but trouble. You sting me and cause me great pain! You've chased away all my family, friends, and visitors. You're nothing but pests to me," said the monstrous human. "And I don't want you or any of your kind around."

Buzzby thought about the lovely house the human had and for an instant he thought of Leezl. "How can you pozzibly be szzo mean when you are szzurrounded by all thizz beauty: the wonderful flowerzz and the szzweet szzmellzz?"

Still puzzled yet more curious, the human said, "I enjoy beautiful things. But I don't enjoy you!"

Buzzby flew around and cautiously circled the human's head. The human twisted its head trying to see Buzzby. Buzzby, remembering his lessons about pollen gathering, pleaded, "Pleazze don't hurt me, I can help you bring beautiful fragrant flowerzz to your garden and cropzz to your barren land. But only if you promizze not to hurt me."

The human paused and seemed intrigued by this offer. "What do you mean? Nothing has grown around here in a long time."

Buzzby gathered more courage, "Let me pollinate a szzmall garden. The flowerzz will grow to be beautiful and szzweet szzmelling for you to enjoy. And your cropzzs will grow plentiful for you to eat."

Hmmm the human pondered then asked inquisitively, "So what you're telling me is that you, a small pesky insect, can bring life to my gardens and land?" The human thought about this for a moment longer, seemingly forgetting he was talking to a bee. As a smile grew, the human said, "Well, I do like lovely fragrant snapdragons and roses. And, of course, tasty squash and cucumbers. Okay, let's see what you can do. I will till the soil, plant the seeds, and do what I do. You pollenate and do what bees do. We'll see how this goes." Pointing a finger at Buzzby, the human said sternly and slowly, "but you can't sting me!"

Then the human did something Buzzby had not expected. "My name is Frank," the human said. "What do they call you?" From a bee's perspective, a self-introduction signaled a desire to foster a pleasant and friendly relationship.

"I'm called Buzzby," he said proudly with his warm cherub-like smile. Buzzby then flew in a pattern recognized by bees as a greeting of peace and friendship, though odd and strange to a human.

During their time together, Buzzby would teach Frank about the important role bees play in the pollination of flowers and vegetables. He explained that as bees collect pollen for food in doing so they transfer pollen from one plant to another. This is how plants produce more flowers and vegetables. He went on to tell Frank that pollen is used to create honey, which is used as a food source. More importantly, bees will only sting as a defense. Frank taught Buzzby about tilling the soil and proper irrigation of the flowers and vegetables. Too much water would drown the plants. Too little does not allow the plants to grow to full maturity. They enjoyed each other's company and growing friendship.

Days turned into weeks and weeks into months. Buzzby had long ago given up hope of a rescue from the soldier bees for surely they had forgotten about him by now. At night while resting from his daily pollen gathering, he often thought of his friends: Leezl, Stinger, and Zeebert, and One-Wing Willie too. He missed them all greatly.

He wondered what they were up to. Did they miss him and did Leezl still think of him. Still, he continued to work with Frank on his garden, pollinating the plants and flowers, and enjoyed learning about humans and teaching the ways of the bee. He especially liked showing Frank how to read a bee's waggle dance talk which are movements used to tell other bees in the hive where to find food sources such as flowers and vegetables.

When Buzzby was not tending to the flowers and vegetables, he exercised his wings and practiced his flight control and waggle dance talk patterns.

Many times Buzzby would accompany Frank to town, often sitting on Frank's shoulder. There, Buzzby learned more about humans. He enjoyed being with his new friend. Buzzby, the once small timid bee had matured. His body had grown fit and trim; his wings, strong and capable; his antenna, long and dark. All quite handsome for a bee. His voice was now deep and steady; he presented an aura of strength and confidence. He took pride in his work and his confidence in flight control had grown to a point he no longer feared a gust of wind.

Late one evening, Frank stepped out from his house and took a deep breath. The sweet smell of flowers filled his lungs. He gazed upon the beauty of the life that now lived in what once was barren soil. A small flower bed and vegetable garden now grew outside his home. Frank was pleased to see

such beauty—the patterns, the colors, the smell of lovely fragrances, and the fresh vegetables.

"Buzzby! We've done it!" Frank said joyfully. "You've brought life back into my garden with this small bed of crocus and daisies. And the cucumbers and squash! I am so thankful for all your work, Buzzby, and even more grateful to learn about bees and their important role in gardening. You've become a true friend."

"You're welcome, Frank," Buzzby replied. "I, too, am quite pleased with our work and our new friendship." Buzzby thought about his time with Frank and how gracious and friendly the former monster turned out to be. Confidently he said, "You know, Frank, if you want, I could get more bees to help grow flowers and vegetables in the vast barren lands between your house and the orchard."

Frank was quite pleased with this idea. "My fields could be productive once again?" he asked Buzzby.

"Yes, Frank. They can be beautiful and plentiful," Buzzby said with a touch of glee. "Frank, now that I know you mean us no harm, I'm confident I could convince the queen to allow us to help you."

With humility and a warm heart Frank said, "I would like that, my little friend. I would like that very much. All bees are welcome here." Happy, though humbled, he expressed, "Buzzby, I had no idea how necessary bees are for the plants and the important part you all play. I am so sorry for the way I acted toward bees before." Buzzby could see the sincerity in Frank's eyes.

With a touch of pride Frank offered, "Buzzby, allow me to give you something. Please give this to your queen as a small token of my offer of friendship to your colony and to all the bees of the orchard." Frank gave Buzzby a small pouch containing pollen from the flowers they worked so hard to grow. Bees view this gesture as a sign of peace and goodwill.

"Thank you, Frank, you are kind and generous. I will be pleased to present this to the queen along with your message of peace and friendship; you will always be a friend to me," Buzzby said with conviction. Buzzby took the pollen and began his flight home; Frank watched sadly as his friend flew away.

Buzzby's flight home was easier now that his wings were strong and his confidence in his flight control was high. He could feel his excitement growing as he approached the edge of the orchard,

especially as he flew over Pollen Plaza. Buzzby flew directly to his hive, hoping he would be remembered. As he arrived, a Sergeant Soldier Bee stopped him near the entrance. An intimidating looking bee with stripes on his wings to indicate his rank shouted, "HALT! Who approaches this hive and what business do you have?"

"I am Buzzby Bee. I have returned from the far side of the barren lands beyond the Edge. I have a special message and a gift for the queen."

The soldier bee paused and looked Buzzby over with a curious eye. "Did you say your name is Buzzby Bee?" inquired the soldier.

Buzzby nodded.

"It's me!" the soldier shouted joyfully. "Me, your old pal Zeebert." The two hovered and embraced and Buzzby was welcomed into the hive. Just inside was Stinger who was coming to visit Zeebert, not knowing Buzzby had returned. Seeing his long-lost friend, Stinger gleefully greeted Buzzby. Zeebert and Stinger proudly paraded Buzzby toward the great hall to see the queen. On their way, Zeebert announced the return of Buzzby Bee to all that could hear.

Stinger, remembering how close Buzzby and Leezl were as youngsters, sensed Buzzby's curiosity about Leezl. Stinger said, "The queen has chosen Leezl to be the queen of a new hive. We're all very excited for the upcoming coronation. I know Leezl will be very happy to see you." Stinger continued to tell Buzzby what had been going on in the hive since his disappearance. He had become an executive pollen trader for the hive. Miss Honey and Captain Comb were now happily married, and sadly, Col. William "One-Wing" Beesly had peacefully passed away.

Though saddened at the passing of the colonel, Buzzby was filled with gladness and pride at the success of his friends and was very excited to reunite with Leezl. They arrived at the great hall where many bees were gathering as the news of his return had spread throughout the hive. The queen sat on a throne with soldier bees of the Royal Guard standing at attention at her sides. Leezl sat near the queen as a princess should.

Zeebert loudly and proudly announced, "Your Majesty, may I present Buzzby Bee. He has returned from beyond the barren lands with an important message and a gift for Her Majesty." The queen, remembering her daughter's long-lost friend, gracefully invited him to come forward. His eyes met Leezl's; their mutual feelings were visible.

Buzzby presented to the queen the pouch of pollen Frank gave to him as a token of peace and goodwill. He told her of his time with the human and how he helped pollinate the flowers and vegetables. He further described how he educated him on bee life and that the human grew kind and generous toward bees. The queen seemed quite interested in Buzzby's experience with the human. She was glad and smiled as Buzzby told her all that he learned from the human, and that his name was Frank. Buzzby also fondly explained to her how he and Frank became friends. He finished his story by informing the queen of Frank's offer to provide safety to all bees of the orchard and that all bees are now welcome to share in the growing fields of flowers and plants in the coming seasons.

50

The queen listened intently to Buzzby's tale contemplating his message. She then stood and announced to all bees in the great hall, "Noble Buzzby Bee, I wish to commend you on your efforts regarding the human called Frank. His token of peace and friendship shall be accepted and honored. Your courage to face him is an inspiration to us all. Your bravery to work with him, educate him in our ways, and befriend him will be held with the highest admiration of this Court and members of this colony."

"As leader of the Council of Queens, I rescind the Royal Rule. From this day forward, all who wish may go to the Edge and beyond and may do so without fear. Buzzby Bee has made it possible for this hive and all hives of this orchard to renew the fields of flowers and vegetables. Let us celebrate the return of Buzzby Bee, the new path of friendship with a human, and the coronation and proclamation of Leezl as queen of a new hive!" The great hall erupted with the roar of cheers and merriment as the bees of the hive began to celebrate.

The queen motioned to Buzzby to step forward. She brought Buzzby and Leezle close to her side. Addressing the two privately she said, "It is with great joy, honor, and pride that I execute my right as queen to give my blessing for you to be at my daughter's side as she becomes queen of the new hive if you both shall choose."

Leezl approached Buzzby who welcomed her with open arms. As they held each other, she whispered in his ear, "I am so happy that you have returned safely to me. I missed you terribly. Buzzby, I would be overjoyed and honored to have you at my side in the new hive. We could bring back the flowers, the bright colors, the sweet smells, and the pollen to feed our hive. We can build our new hive in the great tree, Pollen Plaza. With the help of our friends, members of our colony, and others from the around the orchard, we can rebuild the trade center; the theaters; and the restaurants. We will make it the pride of the orchard, better than it was before. If you accept, we can make these dreams come true."

Filled with warmth and love, Buzzby happily said, "Leezl, I share those dreams. The joy and honor would be mine."

Word spread quickly throughout the orchard of the grand coronation and festival. The Council of Queens, dignitaries, and members from all the colonies of the orchard joined in the celebration. There was a great feast; a banquet of honey and pollen from all parts of the orchard was presented by each hive's master chef. Music was performed by the Royal Bee Band, with other entertainment provided by the Royal Minstrel Flyers.

The day after the celebration, Buzzby and Leezl designated Stinger as the Chief Executive Pollen Trader of the newly reformed Pollen Plaza. They also promoted and commissioned Zeebert as Captain of the Royal Guard, a prestigious position for any Soldier Bee. The two proudly accepted their posts. Miss Honey and Captain Comb were invited to join the new hive as well; she as the school principal and he as the General Soldier Bee. Many other bees gladly accepted the offer to join Leezl and Buzzby to begin building the new hive.

The four friends, united again, led the new colony of bees on their flight to the once terrifying, forbidden tree, Pollen Plaza. There they found a suitable branch to build their new hive overlooking the lands of their new friend, Frank.

As her first official act as queen, Leezl decreed, "No bees of this hive shall sting the human called Frank. We shall all work with him to restore the barren lands and return them to the rich plentiful fields of flowers and vegetables they once were. Buzzby Bee has declared Frank to be his friend, and therefore Frank shall be a friend to us all."

The colony of the new hive immediately began working with Frank to restore the barren lands and ultimately share the abundant beauty and produce with him. As time passed, other hives joined in the reconstruction efforts of Pollen Plaza to once again make it the center of activity for all hives of the orchard.

* * * * * *

It was a cool spring morning at the new hive. Buzzby and Leezl held hands as they enjoyed the renewed activities at Pollen Plaza and the fields beyond. The pollen gathering coordinated by their friend and Executive Pollen Trader, Stinger. The sweet smells of snapdragons, roses, and daisies filled the air. The fields of sunflowers were bright and beautiful. Even in his joy, Buzzby reflected on the wisdom, dedication, and courage of the now departed decorated war veteran Colonel William "One-Wing" Beesly. The revelry of the moment was interrupted by the boisterous happy laughter of the children of the hive who were playing before school. They were teasing their favorite high-ranking soldier bee, Captain of the Royal Guard Zeebert, who was now quick with a joke or two of his own and did not seem to mind these meddlesome youngsters.

CPSIA information can be obtained
at www.ICGtesting.com
Printed in the USA
BVHW020350260220
573344BV00002B/2